MONSTER ACADEMY FOR THE MAGICAL

(MONSTER ACADEMY FOR THE MAGICAL, #1)

JESSICA SORENSEN

AUTHOR'S NOTE

Dear Reader,

Thanks for reading Monster Academy for the Magical (Monster Academy for the Magical, #1). I hope you enjoyed it!

As stated in the book description, Monster Academy for the Magical is a SERIALIZED novella series told in episode form. And I plan to release one episode every 6 to 8 weeks.

Thanks for reading!

Jessica Sorensen

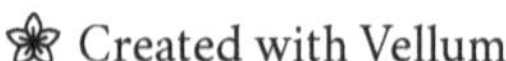 Created with Vellum

PROLOGUE

It was the darkest of nights, no moonlight visible. The sounds of the mother's screams could be heard across the land, sending fear throughout the realm. But the baby's cries overlapped it.

"Help her," the father of the baby whispered.

He wasn't certain if he was talking about his baby or his wife. Well, now that he had seen what sort of creature the baby was, he realized she probably wasn't his. But he could barely process this painful revelation as his wife continued to scream, pulling at her hair, her face pale with exhaustion from giving birth only minutes ago.

The witch doctor still remained in the room, but the rest of the coven had bailed once they laid eyes on the baby, saw what she was, saw the shadows in her eyes.

"A maddening," the doctor whispered in horror as he

backed away from the bloodstained bed where the baby lay beside her mother, kicking and screaming.

The mother had tried to hold the baby at first, despite everyone's fears.

"She won't hurt me," she promised.

But the baby had hurt her. Had made her go mad, poisoned the mother's brain with her power of madness.

"Oh Gods," the father choked out as reality crashed down on him.

His wife had cheated on him. And with a Maddening, one of the most feared and rare creatures in the realms. And now they had a hybrid, half-witch, half-maddening baby on their hands, one that had stolen her mother's sanity within seconds of entering this realm. Not that it was the baby's fault, but…

A rage built inside the husband's chest.

"Get it out of here," he commanded. "Take it as far away from here as possible."

The doctor looked at him with wide eyes. "Sir, I don't think that's possible. You know maddenings can't control their power until they're older. And until then, anyone who tries to touch her is putting themselves at risk for getting cursed by madness."

"Then put a spell on her. Spell her powers to be dormant. I know it's possible to do on younger maddenings." He cast one last glance at the baby and a bit of guilt clutched at his chest.

For months, as the baby grew in his wife's belly, he had fallen in love with the idea of her. Now, though, that love no longer existed. Only hate did. And part of him hated himself for feeling this way, but he couldn't let it go —let go of what the baby represented.

He turned to leave the room.

"After we spell her, where do you want us to take her?" the doctor called out.

He gave a stiff shrug. "I don't care. Just as long as it's far away from here."

"And what about your wife?" The doctor asked cautiously.

His wife let out a scream then, begging for the darkness to leave her.

He ignored her, though, reminding himself that she'd done this to herself.

"Get rid of her. Just make sure I never see her or the baby again," he bit out.

Then he stormed out of the room without so much as a glance back.

The next day, he made a vow to rid his thoughts of the baby and his wife. And for years, he hardly ever thought about them, except on the darkest of nights when no moon was in sight.

When only darkness thrived.

I've always felt like I was... different. Okay, different might be sugarcoating it. Honestly, I've always felt like a freak. Like I can't relate to anyone. Like I don't belong in this world. And sometimes I wonder if maybe, *just maybe,* that's it. If perhaps I don't belong here. If maybe my... curse... ability means I'm from somewhere else. That this curse means I'm something magical. That it means what I did to my first foster mother all those years ago happened because I hadn't learned to control my magic yet.

Back in the day, I thought it was okay to tell people about my secret ability. Boy, was I wrong. This was something I learned the hard way after I told a couple of kids at my school that I believed I had magical powers, that I could sometimes feel magic crawling under my skin and voices whispering to me. I was immediately mocked, ridiculed, and deemed the freak that no one wanted to be around. But honestly, I probably didn't stand a chance anyway, considering what happened all those years ago…

"She was perfectly fine until she showed up," the mother of my foster mother sobbed to the police as her daughter, Mia, was wheeled out on a stretcher…

I remember how Mia had to be strapped down or else she kept trying to claw off her flesh, insisting demons were living inside her. She had also said the same thing about me the first day I was brought to live with her. She had taken one look at my dark, nearly black eyes, and had frowned in disgust. Later, I heard her gossiping with her friends about how I must be possessed like some kid in a movie she had recently watched.

She had pretended it was a joke, but every time she looked at me, I saw the fear in her eyes. It didn't help that I was socially awkward and would barely talk.

And then one stormy night, the… incident happened and now… Well, Mia now spends her days locked in a psych ward.

And me? I do my best not to think about it, think about what I did. But sometimes late at night, it haunts my nightmares.

Maybe I really am a demon.

I've thought this many times, and part of me actually

believes it. Not that I'll ever admit it aloud. Like I said before, I've learned to keep my mouth shut about those sorts of things.

That silence has led to me spending the entire seventeen years of my existence without any friends. While the loneliness can get to me, I've learned to cope with it, learned how to exist by myself without going too mad.

One of the coping mechanisms that have helped me not go insane with loneliness is reading. Books and stories are my escape. Well, normally they are. Right now, though, my love for books may have sentenced me to a horrible punishment.

Earlier today, when I left my house, I thought it'd be okay to make a quick stop at the town book fair. I'd told myself I had plenty of time to hang out there and also have time to run the errands that my newest foster mother had sent me on. I should've known better, remembered how I get around books, how I lose track of time. Now, I'm realizing I never should've stopped and risked being late. It's not like I did—or could've bought— any of the books anyway. I have zero dollars to my name. Always do. Being a foster kid my entire life, I rarely have any money of my own. And with me constantly bouncing through homes, getting a job is complicated. Not that I haven't tried. But no one wants to hire me. That doesn't surprise me since I've spent my entire life aware that most people are repulsed by me.

Even after the incident with Mia was years behind me, I still was the girl no one wanted to be around. Even my teachers acted like I had the plague, although I think some of them had heard the rumors of what I did to Mia. Plus, I'd often zone out during class and go into trances where I wouldn't communicate with anyone. Last year, a rumor was going around that I worshipped the devil. It didn't help that during my zoned-out episodes, I started muttering words in a bizarre language. At least that's what I was told. I can't recollect what happens during my "episodes," as everyone calls them. I only know what people tell me.

A school therapist once suggested I should go see a doctor. My foster parents at the time told her they'd take me to one, but they never did. And I'm glad since the one and only time I talked to a therapist led to me nearly getting put in a "special" group home, which is basically where the send foster kids who are considered danger-ous. I've heard stories about these homes, about the horrible things that go on inside them. It makes living with crappy foster families seem wonderful. Not that all foster parents are that way. I've heard stories about good ones. I just usually seem to end up with the bad ones.

The ones I'm currently living with are the worst. I've been living with them for almost ten months. Ten months of hell.

On the outside, they seem like a nice enough couple.

Middle-aged with no kids of their own, and I'm the only foster kid they're fostering. My first day with them, the foster mother gave me this lecture on how I was basically going to be their maid, that I owed them that for the food and shelter they were going to provide me with. Which whatever. I've been in situations like that before. But what makes this one worse is the punishment system they have for when I mess up. And everything I do seems to be a mess up. Like tardiness, which is about to happen. Again.

As I glance at the time, I quicken my pace to a run. If I hurry, I might be able to make it in time. At least that's what I try to convince myself. Deep down, I know I'm not going to, that I can't run that fast.

Maybe if I try harder, make my feet move quicker—

Smack.

I crash into something solid, the force sending me backward, and I fall all to the ground hard.

"Shit, that hurt," I mutter, blinking up at the object I ran into.

Nope, not an object. A woman with the brightest pink hair I've ever seen, almost like it was spun from magic. Or a cotton candy machine since it looks very similar.

So weird.

She also has on an extravagant black dress secured together with laces and ribbons, and the bottom is made of lace. She looks like she's going to a Halloween party, but it's only September.

"Sorry about that," I tell her as I get to my feet.

Her brows knit. "You can see me?"

"Um... Yeah," I say confusedly. "I just wasn't watching where I was going."

She fiddles with a crescent moon-shaped pendant dangling around her neck as she assesses me with her startling turquoise eyes. "What are you? I can't read you at all? Do you have a shield on you or something?"

And people think I'm crazy?

Deciding to ignore her, I swing to the side to go around her. "Sorry I ran into you," I apologize again, then move to hightail it out of there.

But she reaches out and snags my arm. "Did the coven send you after me? Because I'm not going back." My skin sizzles as she grips my arm. "I won't ever go back to that hellhole." She growls. "I want to stay a huntress. It's what I'm good at. The gift... It bleeds in my bones."

My skin grows so scorching I feel like I'm blistering from the inside out.

What the hell is happening? Who is this person? And what in the crap is she rambling about?

"I don't know what you're talking about." I jerk my arm out of her grasp, and the heat leaves my body. But coldness replaces it, an icy chill glazing inside me. "I'm going to leave now. " I start to walk away when she lets out the most blood-curdling scream I've ever heard.

"Darkness!" She throws her hands over her ears, staring right at me. "You're evil! A monster! Get out of my head!"

And that's about when I say peace out, fleeing the area and running like mad toward my house, leaving Miss Pink Haired Crazy Pants behind. But her screaming chases me for at least another mile.

HAVEN

I'm late. Of course I am. I didn't stand a chance after I ran into that crazy woman. I'm beyond frustrated and kind of weirded out. Yeah, the woman seemed off her rocker, but that's not the first time someone has called me evil or a monster.

I've heard it tons of times. I've just never had a random stranger throw such hate at me before. Did she somehow know about what I did to Mia? It's been years since I crossed paths with someone who remembers that awful day, but it'd explain her reaction to me.

Sort of…

The town clock chimes the next hour, tearing me from my worries and making me focus on another much bigger problem.

Summoning a deep breath, I twist the doorknob and walk into the single-story house that reeks like old shoes.

Tina, my foster mother, is waiting for me in the living room. Her frizzy hair is pulled back into a ponytail, her arms are crossed, and her expression is filled with irritation. But that's just Tina.

"You're late," she says to me with her eyes narrowed. "Tardiness is a sin."

I close the front door behind me.

The curtains are all shut, so the atmosphere is dark—it always is. And the walls are covered in crosses and framed religious quotes. The first time I walked into this house, the sight made me uneasy. I soon learned why, that I could sense the darkness living within these walls.

"Sorry," I tell her as I hand her the sack with flour in it.

She'd sent me to the store to pick it up because her husband had requested biscuits with his dinner tonight. And she always makes him what he requests, I think because she's afraid of him. And she has a good reason to be. The man is a straight-up asshole, evil hidden behind a mask that no one else seems to be able to see.

But I see it. All the damn time.

She snatches the bag from me. "Sorry isn't going to help me get these biscuits done in time, is it?"

"No," I grit my teeth as she glares at me. "I really am

sorry. There was this construction spot, and they had the sidewalk blocked off, so I had to go around it," I try to lie.

"You're such a bad liar." She points a finger at the door that leads to the basement. "Go. Now. And think about your sins."

I ball my hands into fists, fighting back the urge to scream at her. But I want to. Dammit, do I want to. "Please don't make me do this again. I hate… I hate the dark. It makes me anxious." That part is true.

It started the day I hurt Mia. Darkness had been a big part of that day—had been all of it.

Memories of that day try to surface, but I shove them back, refusing to remember what happened—what I did.

"You know the rules," Tina snaps, continuing to point at the door. "Tardiness is a sin in this house."

Everything is a sin in this house.

Stabbing my fingernails into my palms, I march over to the door, yank it open, and step in. A lamp is on at the bottom of the stairway, but it's still extremely dark. But I don't bother turning the light on. I've had this punishment enough to know she's about to shut off the breaker, so I have no choice but to sit in the dark. So I rush down the steps before the lights go off to avoid falling down them, something that happened the first time I was sentenced to this punishment. I ended up cutting open my arm on a nail and still have a scar from it.

The moment I reach the bottom of the staircase, I

hurry toward a recliner. It's where I sit while I'm down here. Halfway there, though, the lamps goes off and darkness smothers me.

"Dammit." I squint against the darkness, trying to see something, but no windows are around to offer even a drop of light, so I'm left trying to mentally visualize my surroundings.

I know a shelf is on my left, and to my right, is a wall. And I think just a few steps forward is where the recliner is.

Sticking out my hands, I stumble through the darkness until the fronts of my legs bump into the recliner. I sink down onto the chair, hug my knees against my chest, and keep my gaze in the direction of what I hope is the stairway, waiting and watching.

Waiting and watching for the other half of my punishment to come.

For *him* to come for me.

HAVEN

I'm unsure how much time goes by since I don't own a phone. I do have an old watch I found in a parking lot once. I have it on right now, but it's too dark to see the time. I can hear it ticking, though, taunting me. The noise is maddening, and I find myself longing to hear something else—anything else.

But the moment I hear another noise, I wish I could go back to listening to the clock tick.

Here he comes.

I hate him.

I don't want to do this again.

What I would give to just vanish.

Or be able to fight back for once—

A sliver of light pierces through the darkness as he opens the door at the top of the stairway. Vomit burns in my throat as footsteps descend the stairs, slowly but with purpose.

"Oh Haven," Tim, my foster father, taunts me as he reaches the bottom of the stairs.

I curl further into the shadows, trying to become one with them. But he finds me. He always does.

"I heard you misbehaved today," he says to me as he stands in front of the recliner with his arms crossed, the light from upstairs drifting down and hitting against his back.

I smash my lips together, stupidly hoping that he can't see me. That maybe these strange abilities of mine will suddenly make a grand appearance again and make me invisible.

"So we're going to play the silent game, huh?" He starts to remove his belt. "Good. That means I won't have to hear you cry this time."

I bite down on my tongue so hard I taste blood.

He laughs darkly, the sound sending goosebumps across my flesh. "You're amusing when you're scared… Like a frightened little bird." He gets his belt all the way off, wraps it around his hand, then reaches for me.

I dart to the side, hopping off the recliner. Then I run. But he shoves me to the side, and I fall down, smacking my head against the concrete floor.

For a strange as hell moment, I swear I feel hot again

like I did earlier when the crazy pink-haired woman grabbed me.

Scorching.

I'm melting from the inside.

Part of me wishes I'd start on fire and take this whole damn house down with me.

But when dizziness consumes me, that heat stifles.

I stumble to my feet, but my head pulsates, and I collapse back to the floor. Blood roars in my eardrums as darkness swarms my vision. It feels like I'm about to be swallowed up by something.

Part of me wishes it would happen.

And then I feel it. That cold sensation I feel whenever I zone out.

Not right now, please, I beg my mind. If I black out, I won't know what he does to me. Then again, I hate thinking about what he's done to me, how he's hurt me, tied me up with that stupid belt and touched me. I have scars on my wrist from that belt. And scars in my mind from what he's done to me.

I hate this.

I hate that I'm too weak to fight him off.

Hate that out of everyone I've ever crossed paths with, he's the one who decided he wasn't afraid to be near me.

I hate this.

Hate this life.

Hate how weak I am.

For collapsing moment, I feel like just giving up.

"Just give up, Haven," he whispers in my ear. "Stop fighting."

No!

That fire blazes through me again, potent and toxic. *Powerful.*

Sucking in a breath, I push to my feet.

I won't give up.

I won't!

But he places his foot onto my back, pinning me down against the floor.

"Get off me," I growl out, tears burning my eyes like the heat searing inside my body.

Why am I so hot?

He pushes down on me harder, and I feel him lean over me.

"You always smell so good," he whispers, sniffing my hair again. "Like fear and weakness. Two of my favorite things." He takes one more breath then roughly grabs my wrists and pins them behind my back.

I open my mouth to scream, even though I know it won't do any good. I've screamed before and Tina never comes, so she's well aware of what her husband does to me, and she just chooses to ignore it.

But I refuse to go down without a fight, so I scream until I become hoarse, until I'm crying, until Tim has me tied up, until his hands are touching me.

I hate him.

I wish I could hurt him.

I wish I could make him pay.

I want to make him burn.

I want to let the darkness swallow him whole.

I want to take over his mind and devour it.

Those crazy thoughts are the last I have before darkness takes over my mind and sweeps me away.

HAVEN

My new foster mother won't stop telling everyone that I'm tainted. I'm not even sure what tainted means, but everyone seems to be afraid of me whenever she tells them this.

I wish she'd stop it, wish she'd see that there's nothing wrong with me.

Sure, I look and act a bit different. My eyes are really dark, and I always feel disconnected whenever I'm talking to someone. I don't know why I'm this way, but I don't do it on purpose. I just don't know how to act.

But I'm trying, like right now.

I'm sitting in the kitchen with one of Mia's friend's daughter. Her name is Lea, and she has blond hair and blue eyes; normal blue eyes that I'm envious of. Everyone is always afraid of my eyes.

"Your eyes are really scary," Lea tells me as she stuffs a handful of candy into her mouth. "It's probably why your parents didn't want you."

I swallow hard, wanting to scream at her, but if I do, I know I'll get in trouble. "No, that's not why."

She smirks. "Really? Then why did they get rid of you?"

I lift a shoulder, staring at the linoleum floor. I hate talking about my parents. It hurts for some reason.

She laughs. "I bet it was because of your eyes. And you're really weird. My older brother said he heard my mom and your fake mom talking about how you're like probably possessed by some sort of evil spirit."

I say nothing and part of me likes it that way, likes not talking. But the other part of me wants to yank on her hair hard enough to make her cry.

"Are you?" she sneers as she stuffs another handful of candy into her mouth.

"Am I what?" I ask.

She grins and candy is stuck to her teeth. "Are you evil? Maybe that's why your parents didn't want you. Because you are. And you're ugly, so maybe that's why too. Or maybe they're just bad people... Or maybe they hate you. Or maybe they're killers—"

Something snaps inside me, and I reach out and pull her hair.

She lets out a scream. "Get away from me!"

I immediately let go of her hair. "S-sorry," I sputter.

But she keeps screaming.

A few seconds later, my foster mother and Lea's mother come rushing into the kitchen.

Lea is in tears by then, and all I want to do is run.

"What did you do?" Mia snaps, glaring at me.

I open my mouth to admit what I did, but Lea cries out, "She tried to beat me up! And she said she was going to kill me!"

"I did not!" I cry out, shaking my head, tears burning in my eyes.

Mia's glare deepens as she grabs my arm, her fingernails digging into my skin as she yanks me to my feet. "I should've listened to my instincts about you." She drags me toward the living room. "I should've told them to take you back the moment I saw you."

Tears sting in my eyes. "I didn't do anything!" I shout, trying to defend myself.

"Liar!" she shouts, shoving me down on the sofa. "You're nothing but a liar."

"No, I'm not—"

She strikes me across the face, shocking both of us. For a moment, she pauses, staring at me with wide eyes. But then she collects herself and strikes me again. And again. And again. As pain builds inside me, so does this strange heat.

Sweltering.

I feel so hot.

I hear voices from somewhere. Mia screaming, I think. And

then I hear nothing. Nothing but the soft chants of something that can only be described as madness.

When I regain consciousness, I'm lying face down on the cold basement floor, my wrists are untied, and the air is quiet. But it's a maddening sort of silence. One good thing, though, is that the heat I felt in my body is gone. A chill is now glazing through my veins, but it feels soothing. Just like the quiet.

Then I hear a noise, mumbling from somewhere, and that soothing sensation shatters.

I gulp. *Oh God, this is just like the incident with Mia.*

But who's mumbling? Tim? Probably. But I'm not about to stick around and find out.

I need to get out of here.

I jump to my feet, but instantly regret it as my head throbs and the room spins. I blink several times, struggling to keep my balance—

The lights click on and I stiffen.

Crap. Crap. Crap.

Squinting against the light, I frantically peer around. Everything appears normal, except Tim isn't anywhere. That mumbling, though, it has to be him. It sounds just like when I unleashed my powers on Mia.

"Where the hell is he?" I mumble as I take a cautious

step forward—

"Oh my God, what have you done!" Tina cries out from behind me.

I spin around and find her looking beneath the stairway, her face pale as death, her eyes wide in horror.

Every part of me screams *run*!

I reel around toward the stairway, preparing to get the hell away from this house. I don't care if I get called in as a runaway again. It'll be better than living in this hellhole.

"Get over here right now!" Tina screams at me, grabbing the back of my shirt.

She jerks on me hard enough that I stumble back, and my gaze zeroes in underneath the stairway. I freeze as terror rips through me.

I hadn't really gotten a good look at Mia after I had accidentally used my powers on her. Too many people had been there and had gotten in my way. Plus, Lea's mom had shouted for me to get out of the house, so I had left. Only I didn't know where to go, so I ended up sitting on the front porch until the cops showed up.

Part of me has always wondered what exactly happened to Mia, what she looked like as she chanted that language no one seemed to recognize. But if she looked at all like Tim, I'm glad I didn't see it at the time, because the sight is absolutely horrifying.

He's cowering underneath the stairway with his hands

over his ears, the blood veins on his arms so prominent they look like they're about to pop out from underneath his skin.

That heat in my body builds again, a voice filling my head.

Look at what you've done.

I shake my head. "I didn't do this." But really, I know I did.

Tina jabs a finger in my face. "Yes, you did! You did this to him! I know you did! You sick freak of nature! You sinner," she hisses, leaning close to me. "I knew you were a bad seed from the moment I laid eyes on you. I should've sent you back! I should've listened to the rumors about you!"

"I didn't do this to him," I say in an uneven tone. "How could I… I mean, what even happened to him?"

Deep down, I know. Know that somewhere, deep inside me a darkness lives. I don't know why I have it in me or where it comes from. All I know is that I just unleashed it on Tim.

I wanted to hurt him.

Wanted to make him pay.

Take his mind and devour it, I had thought.

And I did.

I just don't know how.

I inhale shakily. "I didn't do this—"

Tina shoves me back so hard I slam into the wall. "You

did!" she shouts as she storms for the stairway. "I'm calling the police. You're going to jail where sinners like you belong."

"But I didn't do anything!" I cry out, rushing up the stairs after her.

When she reaches the top of the stairway, she slams the door in my face and locks me in. Locks me in the darkness again. Only this time I'm not haunted by the quietness. No, I have Tim's rambling to fill up the silence.

Sinking down onto the stairs, I lower my head into my hands and try to remember what happened. But my memories become hazy after Tim tied up my wrists with his belt. I have no idea how I got out of that and if he touched me or not. And I have no idea what led up to Tim being under the stairs, rambling to himself in some sort of different language. But I have a feeling that when the police show up, I'll get blamed for this. Not that it'll be official. With Mia, there was only speculation that turned into rumors around town.

What if this time, though, they find a way to blame this on me? Then what, Haven?

I swallow hard, wondering what waits for me when the police show up, what Tina will tell them I did. She's a good liar, and I worry she'll come up with quite the story that makes me look extremely guilty. And unlike the incident with Mia, I'm seventeen years old now, not legally an adult, but close enough that I might get in trouble.

Although, I'm not sure what I'll get in trouble for. Tim's condition is… well, really weird, but very similar to Mia's condition. What if they put two and two together and figure out just how much of a freak I am? That I have these strange abilities connected to darkness?

Maybe I can just tell the police about what Tim does to me in the darkness of this basement. Then again, in the past, whenever I've tried telling someone that my foster parents were hurting me, no one believed me.

What if they don't believe me now?

What if I'm going to jail?

What's going to happen to me?

Those thoughts haunt my mind until the sounds of sirens overlap Tim's mumbling. A few minutes later, the basement door opens up. Tina appears in the doorway along with two uniformed officers.

"She's the one who did it," she tells one of the officers as she points a finger at me. "She… broke my husband."

I stand up and shake my head. "I didn't do anything. I swear I didn't… He just… He went crazy."

"Liar!" Tina shouts, her face red. "She hurt my Tim. She's the reason he…" She doesn't finish her sentence, standing there with a dumbstruck look on her face.

Her accusation is enough for one of the officers to haul me out of the house. When we get outside, he puts me in the back of his vehicle, arresting me for… Well, whatever the hell happened to Tim.

Okay, apparently just because you get put in the back of a police car, doesn't mean you're actually being arrested, something I learn after the officer returns and lets me out of the back of his vehicle.

An ambulance has arrived by then, and neighbors are crowding around the yard. As I stand near the police vehicle, trying to ignore the stares, the officer informs me that the paramedics believe Tim is suffering from a mental breakdown. He asks me a bunch of questions, like why we were in the basement to begin with, and what events took place that led up to Tim mentally breaking.

Part of me wants to tell him the truth, tell him about all the times I've been locked in that basement. Tell him how Tim would come down there and tie me up, then touch me against my will. But just the thought of saying all this aloud sends fear and self-disgust coursing my body.

I hate that I feel this way. So weak.

I've always been so weak.

Instead, I end up telling the officer that when I walked into the basement to do some laundry, I found Tim in the condition he's in now. The officer doesn't seem very satisfied by my answer, but when I insist several times that I'm telling the truth, he gives up and goes over to talk to Tina, who's sobbing beside the stretcher Tim is being wheeled out on.

When the paramedics put Tim in the back, he starts screaming words that make no sense. Tina sobs harder as she moves to duck into the back with him. Right before she gets in, though, she glances at me.

"You're going to hell for this! You... monster!" Tears flood her eyes, and hatred burns in her tone.

And I have to wonder if she's right. If I am going to hell for this.

If I am a monster.

After the ambulance pulls away, I'm told that my time with Tina and Tim has come to an end. Not that I didn't expect that already. And I'm glad. Although, I'm a bit stressed out over where I'll end up next. But honestly, at this point, I'm just grateful I didn't get arrested.

A few hours later, I've packed up all of my stuff, and the police put me in a vehicle to take me down to social services so they can hand me over to my caseworker.

We arrive only minutes later, and I find myself wishing the drive was longer because my social worker is… Well, let's just say not very nice.

Her name is Beth, and she has what people call a resting bitch face. The expression is fitting too since she can be a real bitch sometimes.

"You know, I wish I could say I'm not surprised you made yet another one of your foster parents have a psychotic breakdown," she tells me after the police officer has filled her in on what happened. "But I'm not." She shuts my file and overlaps her hands on top of it. "You've been in the system for seventeen years, basically since you were born. Most babies who get put into the system end up getting adopted. But you… you were trouble even when you were in diapers. And your record…" She shakes her head, her bitch face in full form. "Stealing, lying, causing trouble, scaring everyone… And now this…" She gives another shake of her head. "Do you know how complicated it's going to be to place you in a home now? It was already bad enough…" She sighs. "How did you even cause that poor man to have a breakdown?"

"I didn't," I mutter, fiddling with the leather bands I keep on my wrist to hide the scars caused Tim gave me from tying me up with that damn belt.

The way the scars look, people always assume I put then there myself. That I'm either a cutter or suicidal. Tim and Tina used that to their benefit, told everyone stories about how they found me in the bathroom cutting my wrist with a razor blade. Whenever I tried to defend myself, they'd punish me. So eventually, I learned to keep my mouth shut.

"Maybe you did. Maybe you didn't. Honestly, you lie so much I don't know what to believe anymore." She sighs again. "You're just lucky you can't get charged for causing someone to have a nervous breakdown."

"I didn't do anything, Beth," I insist, but the words *liar, liar* whisper through my mind. "I swear I didn't."

She shakes her head. "That'd be easier to believe if this wasn't the first time you've caused trouble, but it's not. You're one of my most troubled cases. I'm honestly surprised Tim and Tina even took you in. And now..." She lets out an exasperated sigh.

I bite down on my tongue, wanting to scream in frustration. But I resist the urge, knowing she's right. I have gotten into a lot of trouble over the years, have caused a lot of breakdowns.

You're a liar.

No one wants you.

You're a monster.

As an overwhelming loneliness overcomes me, I hug my backpack against my chest. It contains all of my belongings; a few outfits, my journal, a couple of books, and a locket that was left with me when my mother—or father—left me at the fire station only a few days after I was born. No one knows who my parents are, why they abandoned me, or even when my real birthday is. I had nothing with me other than a blanket, the basket that I was in, and that locket. That's it. There wasn't even a photo in the locket. Just a piece of paper that had *Haven Wyllowravelee* written on it. Everyone assumed that was my name, but no one could ever find any records of me being born, or linking me to anyone who could be my parents, like I was some sort of alien dropped into the world. Maybe that's what I am. I don't know, though, besides my weird ability, odd personality, and freaky eyes, everything else about me seems normal. I can bleed, get hurt, scar. In fact, I scar really easily.

Still, I can't stop thinking about where I come from and why I am the way I am. Sometimes I find myself making up stories in my head about why my parents dropped me off at the station. Maybe my mom was running from bad people and thought it'd be the only way I'd be safe. Maybe both my parents were killed, and someone else left me there. Deep down, though, I know those kinds of stories probably aren't what really happened. That more than likely my parents just didn't want me, just like Lea said.

"At this point, I'm not even sure where to place you," Beth continues on, interrupting my internal pity party. "With your file and you being seventeen… It's hard to place seventeen-year-olds as it is."

"So I'm going to a group home again?" I ask, a bit of relief washing over me.

Sure, group homes suck balls, but the idea of moving in with another foster family, of not knowing what kind of family I'll get placed with… my stomach churns just thinking about it. At least in a group home, I'm less likely to have to deal with Tims. Although, group homes come with their own complications, but still…

I think I need a break from living with adults.

"Unfortunately, I don't think we have another option right now," Beth replies, reaching for her phone. "Go wait out in the waiting room while I make some calls and find out which home can take you in."

Nodding, I leave her office and get comfortable in the waiting area, which is vacant since it's Sunday. Since this isn't my first rodeo, I know it could take Beth hours to get me set up in a group home. Thankfully, I have some books I can read.

But I barely get one out when Beth strolls into the waiting room.

"Good news, Haven." She smiles at me. Actually freakin' smiles, something I've never seen her do in the years I've known her. "I've managed to get you into a special group home that focuses on unique teenagers like you."

"Um… okay." Her smile is freaking me out, but I do my best not to stare at it. "What do you mean by unique?" *God, please don't let this be one of those group homes for dangerous kids.*

"Special," she explains while continuing to smile at me like a possessed maniac.

If I didn't know any better, I'd swear she was possessed.

Or the pink crazy-haired woman in disguise, like she body-snatched Beth or something.

I mentally shake my head at that thought. *Why would you think that, Haven? That kind of shit doesn't exist.*

Right?

I don't know… considering what I can do…

I eyeball Beth over. "Is everything okay?"

She gives a cheerful nod. "This is going to be good for you. This place… I think you'll fit in well there." She tugs at the sleeves of her button-down shirt. "They'll be picking you up in about an hour. While you wait, maybe you should go clean up a bit."

Since when does she tell me to clean up?

"You're not taking me there?" In the ten odd years I've

known her, she's always driven me to the group home and checked me in.

She shakes her head. "Like I said, this is a special group home." She snaps her fingers, signaling for me to go to the bathroom. "Now go clean up. I don't want them showing up and seeing you like this. They might take back your spot if they do."

Swallowing hard, I collect my bag, get up and head into the bathroom, creeped out at how I can feel her watch me the entire way, only looking away when I push into the bathroom.

"She's acting so weird," I mutter to myself as I make my way over to the mirror/sink area.

I cringe the instant I catch sight of my reflection, realizing why Beth told me to clean up.

My long, dark hair is a tangled mess, and my nearly black eyes are bloodshot, which makes them look even creepier. I also have dirt all over my cheeks, and a couple of droplets of bloodstain the front of my grey T-shirt.

Where the hell did the blood come from?

I check my arms and face over. Then my legs. Since I'm wearing shorts, I get a good look at how badly my knees are scraped up, old blood crusted on my flesh. Maybe that's where the blood came from, but how did it get on my shirt? It doesn't make sense.

I lift up my shirt to check my stomach, and my heart slams to a stop. Moving across my flesh are what appear to be blood veins, prominent and protruding like they're about to pop out of my skin.

Just like Tim's were.

But when I blink, my skin returns to normal.

"What the actual hell?" I mutter as I run my fingers across my now smooth flesh.

Well, this is definitely new. But I'm not sure what to make of it, other than maybe I'm losing my mind.

Maybe I'm going crazy. Perhaps that's why I'm going to this special group home. Maybe special means for the insane. Or perhaps they're sending me to a mental institution. Or maybe I am going to that group home for dangerous kids.

I swallow hard then start to scrub the dirt off my face. Then I change my shirt and comb my fingers through my hair. My shoelaces are untied, but I'm too exhausted to bend down and tie them.

I just want to leave, escape all of this.

As I exit the bathroom, I debate whether I should make a run for it. I've run away before, but I've always gotten caught a day or two later. Still, I'd rather try then just let them take me to this "special" group home—

I slap to the stop as shock unexpectedly whips through me. "What the hell is that?" I whisper as I stare at the... well, I'm not sure what the swirling circle of darkness in front of me is.

I start to step back into the bathroom, unsure what else to do when Beth appears beside me.

"Your ride has arrived, Haven." She gives me that manic smile again, and a chill slithers down my spine.

I trip backward, trying to get away from her, but she snatches hold of my arm, her smile broadening. Then, as if a veil has been lifted from her, she shifts from looking like a middle-aged, grey-haired woman to a twenty-something-year-old gothic chick with cotton candy pink hair.

My eyes widen. "You're the crazy woman I ran into earlier."

"Not a woman. *A witch.*" She grins. "And you're a maddening, which means you shouldn't be here. Luckily, I found you before something else did. Evil or not, you need to be protected. And don't worry about being a monster. Where you're going, monsters are accepted. And they'll protect you there."

I barely register her words before she shoves me forward toward the swirling circle of darkness.

"Hey! What the hell!" I shout as I attempt to regain my balance.

But I end up tripping over my shoelaces.

Dammit, I should've laced them.

I didn't, though, and now I'm stumbling straight into the vortex.

Into the darkness.

That I'm pretty sure might lead to Hell.

*D*arkness, darkness everywhere.
Surrounding me.
Pulling me down.
Into the pits of hell—
Swoosh.

I fall out of the vortex and land on a shiny black marble floor. But I don't land very gracefully and my legs giving out on me. I trip forward, nearly landing on my face. Luckily, I get my hands out in time or else I may have broken my face.

"Well, that was close." Relief trickles through me until I remember that I just fell out of a vortex that I'm pretty sure leads to hell.

Shit, am I in Hell?

I quickly stumble to my feet, adjusting my backpack,

my gaze skimming along the massive black columns lining the grey walls. Above me is a domed ceiling painted with a mural of a woman with glitter silver skin, and snakes and flames surround her. Pieces of embers float in the air and smoke swirls around me.

"Yeah, I'm definitely in Hell," I mutter, turning in a circle, trying to figure out if I'm hallucinating.

Logically, it seems like I am, yet everything feels so real, as if I'm just waking up from a seventeen-year dream and finally entering reality.

What doesn't seem real, though, is how unafraid I am.

I should be freaking out, right? I mean, some crazy woman… or well, witch as she told me…

I stop my thoughts right there. *Witches don't exist.*

Then again, what I did to Tim and Mia shouldn't exist either.

"Holy crap, did I really meet a witch?" I mutter, deciding I must be in shock or something. That has to be the reason I'm not freaking out that… "I'm in Hell."

"Oh no, honey, this isn't hell, I assure you." A crackling voice sails over my shoulder.

I startle, spinning around, only to be startled again by a person… creature… whatever it is that's standing in front of me.

It's tall, even compared to my five foot ten height. Where its hair should be, flames blaze instead, smoke funnels from its eye sockets, and its flesh singes like embers. Weirdly, it's wearing a pair of nice black pants, and a shirt, vest, and tie, all formal attire. Nice looking even.

"You know, Hell being all fire and smoke is a complete misconception." The creature informs me with a glowing smile. "Don't get me wrong. There is a lot of fire there, but some of us fire demons got together about a century ago and decided to spruce it up a bit. We put up a big rainbow in front of the Death Pit and even dazzled up the smoky sky with a bit of pink starlight. It can be really pretty at night. Well, if you can get past the stench of burning flesh." He thrums his finger against his lips. "I haven't figured out a way to cover up that smell yet. One day, though, I'll figure it out." He blinks from his thinking trace and focuses on me. "But anyway, on behalf of Monster Academy for the Magical, I'd like to welcome you to your new home for the next year." He snaps his fingers, and a handheld device appears in his palm. "Let me just look at your file and see which office I need to take you to to check you in." He starts humming a tune under his breath as he reads something on the screen of the device.

Me? I just stand there, completely dumbstruck and fully convinced I'm dead. Or in some sort of trance induced nightmare.

I pinch myself then wince. *Shit, that hurt.*

"Aw, here it is," the… fire demon—at least that's what

he called himself—says. "Mary T. Starford, daughter of Jill and Alford, two of those most powerful witches in all the realms, and who happened to be graduates of Monster Academy for the Magical." He smiles proudly. "Not that we like to take full credit for our pupils' achievements, but we'd like to think the academy played a part in their success."

"I…" Witches? Monster Academy? What the… I struggle to find words so I can tell him I have no damn clue what's going on, but I can't get anything coherent to leave my lips.

"What is it, honey?" The fire demon asks with concern. "Are you nervous? If so, maybe I can get my hands on a bit of relaxation potion."

I shake my head. *Just spit it out.* "My name's not Mary T. Starford."

Okay, that's a start.

Frowning, he returns his attention to the screen. "Are you sure?" Smoke hisses from his fingers as he scratches his head. "Because I'm not supposed to have another arrival today."

"Yeah, I'm sure." This time my voice comes out a bit more even.

"Okay." Confusion cracks in the embers covering his forehead as he looks back at me. "The files must've gotten mixed up. While we have it pretty together around here, mistakes do sometimes happen, thanks to everything running on technology these days."

His words remind me of this cranky man I lived with for a couple of weeks about four years ago. He hated anything that had to do with technology and was always ranting about it. But he wasn't too bad of a person, and I wouldn't have minded living with him permanently. Sadly, though, he died of a heart attack not too long after I was placed with him.

But what I find strange that his and the fire demon's words match up so well. Maybe I'm having a *Wizard of Oz* moment. Maybe I'm currently lying on the floor of the waiting room at social services, passed out and dreaming.

"What's your name?" the fire demon asks, drawing me from my thoughts.

I swallow down a shaky breath and will my voice to come out even. "Haven Wyllowravelee."

His confusion doubles, just like the cracks in his skin. "And what is your power?"

"I…" *What?* "Um… I don't have one." *Do I?*

I think about what I did to Tim and Mia.

But what sort of power is that?

He gives me a tolerant look. "Nice try. But I've heard better excuses to try getting out of going here. I don't know why you newbies freak out during your arrival here. It's not that bad. I mean, sure, it does kind of has that whole demon lair vibe going in this area," he gestures around the room. "But this is just the entryway."

"I'm not trying to get out of here," I insist, although that might be a lie—I'm not really sure how I feel at the moment. "I really don't know what my power is. I don't even know why I'm here… Or where here is."

Tension flashes across his face. "What realm did you enter here from?"

"I… um… The human one?" It comes out sounding more like a question.

When his expression dims, I know I've given a wrong answer to his question.

"Oh dear." The smoke stops funneling from his eyes, leaving me to stare at the gaping holes where his eyeballs should be. "I've never had to deal with this kind of situation before," he mumbles as he glances at the handheld device. He's quiet for a crackle of a moment, and then smoke slowly starts to pour from his eyes again. "I think I need to take you to the main dungeon."

My eyes widen as I step back. "Um, no thanks. I think I'll just go home."

But what is home, Haven? You don't have one. You're supposed to be in a group home right now. Or, well, that's what Beth said. But Beth turned into a pink-haired woman who shoved me into this vortex so…

He gives me a funny look. "Relax. The main dungeon is where all the new students go to check in. Not that you're a new student, but the headmistress and headmaster might have a better idea of what to do with you." He ambles toward a set of tall, blood red doors at the far end of the room. "Come along, honey." He snaps his fingers at me, signaling for me to follow him.

Seeing no other option, I muster up every ounce of courage I have and follow him toward the door, still not fully convinced this place isn't Hell.

On the other side of the doors is a wide hallway that seemingly goes on for miles. Lanterns light up the way, black and red tiles pave the floor, and flames cover the ceiling, yet the air is strangely cold.

We don't remain in the hallway for very long before the fire demon comes to a stop in front of another set of tall, red doors. He opens them up and ushers me inside. Then he walks in behind me, letting the doors close.

I'm not sure what I expected a main dungeon to look like, but this is definitely not it. Like the room I entered this place in, black columns line the dark grey walls, but the ceiling is covered in massive chandeliers, and what can only be described as intricately carved thrones line the room. And at the center of it all is a massive ebony desk and sitting behind it is a woman with sun orange hair is talking on what looks to be an old school antique phone.

She's not the only... person in the room either. Some thrones are occupied by... people? Honestly, I'm not sure what any of them are, since all of them have either glittery skin, horns, or in some cases, scales.

"Come along." The fire demon signals for me to follow him as he starts up the path toward the desk. "Let's go see if we can figure out why you were sent here."

Adjusting my backpack, I trail after him, trying not to gawk at the people... creatures as I pass by them, worried the whole staring-is-rude police applies to this place too. But I fail big time as my gaze falls on a large, hairy beast-like creature with hooves for feet and eyeballs sprouting out of its head.

What the actual crap is that?

As if sensing my gaze, the beast grunts and blows smoke into my face that reeks so badly that I gag.

"Dude, it's like she's never seen a seeing a demon before," a male voice drifts from somewhere nearby.

It has a musical sound, almost hypnotic, and my gaze magnetizes to it, leading me to a guy sitting beside the beast. He's watching me in amusement, and he looks around my age with sky blue hair and unnaturally looking, but incredibly gorgeous crimson lips. He's wearing a pair of dark pants, a button-down short-sleeved grey shirt, and the look is topped off with a thin tie. While his features seem human-like, his prettiness factor makes him appear otherworldly. And his eyes… They actually sparkle like rubies.

Pretty…

As I continue to stare at him, attempting to figure out what he is, his lips tug into a cocky smile, revealing his perfectly straight … *fangs?*

I blink in shock, which elicits a chuckle from him. Then he runs his tongue along his teeth, and his eyes flash red as if he's hungry.

Blood hungry.

Holy effing hell. Is he a vampire?

This has to be a dream…

I almost pinch myself again, but I'm too busy staring.

"Stop trying to scare her, Phoenix," a guy sitting beside him mutters. "We were warned about tormenting the newbies."

His angelic voice should help me relax, except the guy looks anything but angelic, dressed head to toe in black, chains dangle from his belt loops, leather bands cover his wrists, and his inky black hair hangs in his stormy grey eyes that are currently locked on me.

He briefly assesses me with mild curiosity before fixing his attention on the front desk.

"She looks too old to be a newbie," Phoenix remarks, glancing at the guy next to him.

"Yeah, well, maybe she's a late enrollment because she

looks way too scared not to be new," he says in a bored tone.

I'd take his words offensively, but I'm too stuck on the fact that shadows are starting to ripple across his skin.

"Maybe." Phoenix fixes his gaze back on me. "Are you a newbie?"

It takes me a moment to realize he's talking to me.

I'm about to reply when another guy comes rushing by me and plops down in the throne beside the guy with shadows on his skin.

He looks around the same age as the other guys, has short, blonde hair, pale blue eyes, and a shimmery glow radiates from him.

"You're late, Ollie," the shadowy guy informs him with a heavy sigh.

Ollie trades an amused smile with Phoenix then reclines back in the throne. "Sorry, boss," he jokes with a smirk. "But I promise it was for a good reason." When the guy with shadows on his skin stares him down, his head bobs back and lets out a groan. "Roman, chill out. No one noticed I was a few minutes late." A smile plays at his lips. "Besides, it was for an excellent reason."

"Hooking up Debbie G. in the janitor's closet isn't a good reason," The guy with shadows on his skin—Roman replies with a shake of his head.

"Actually, it was Debbie G. and Stephanie S." Ollie

smirks, tucking his hands behind his head and seeming pretty pleased with himself.

But that pleased look morphs into confused curiosity as his gaze zeroes in on me.

He leans forward, resting his hands on his knees. "Well, well, what do we have here?" His pale blue eyes skim up and down my body then his smile grows. "Fresh meat."

And just like that, the spell I seem to have fallen into is broken.

Fresh meat? Is he kidding me?

"Actually, we were just trying to figure that out," Phoenix tells him while grinning at me. "She never answered my question, though."

"Just leave her alone," Roman mutters, pinching the brim of his nose. "You should both realize by now that messing around with newbies only leads to clinginess." He throws them both pressing looks.

Ollie sighs. "Yeah, you're probably right." He glances at me again. "Such a shame, though. Those eyes and those legs…" He bites down on his bottom lip.

"She's easily tranced too," Phoenix adds with a grin. "So either she's weak or stupid. I can't figure out which one."

And that's about when I become aware that I've been standing in the same place for who knows how long, listening to these guys talk about me as if I was watching a show. And as I realize that, a haze begins to lift from me, my mind clearing, and everything they said sinking in.

I blast them with a dirty look. "Screw you. I'm not stupid. And I'm not weak." It might be the boldest thing I've ever done.

If only that sort of bravery existed while I was in the… Well, wherever I was before I came here.

Wanting to latch onto that confidence, I lift my chin and step away, catching a glimpse of their shocked expressions. Why they're the ones who are shocked, though, I don't have a clue. They're the ones who seem perfectly comfortable in this place that screams of nightmares.

HAVEN

By the time I arrive at the front desk, I feel like I just got high and am coming down. I have a suspicion it has to do with those guys... Or whatever the hell they are.

The fire demon greets me with an amused smile as I wander up to stand beside him. "I see you've met Phoenix, Roman, and Ollie."

"Yeah... Well, not really met... Just stared at them." I have the craziest urge to peek over my shoulder at them, but resist the temptation. "How'd you know?"

He grins, smoke slipping from his lips. "Because you look a little dazed, which can mean only one of two things. One," he holds up a finger, "You accidentally smoked some dream smoke, which is currently restricted here. So that only leaves option number two," he holds up another finger, "And that's that you got hazed by the Death Triplets. Although they're not really triplets. But that's the nickname they've been given."

My brows rise. "The Death Triplets? For reals?"

"Yeah, it's what everyone around here calls those three over there." He points in the direction of the guys, but I still don't glance at them. "Not that most don't mind getting hazed by them. They're ridiculously hot." He dazes off with a dreamy look in his eyes.

"What does hazed mean exactly?" I ask. "Like hazing in college?"

"Nah, it's just a thing they do. They're all considered alluring creatures so when they combine their powers, they can basically trance creatures into a lust stupor. Or a haze, hence the nickname."

"I…" I shake my head as my brain struggles to process what he just said.

Frowning, the fire demon's lips part. "I think…" He sighs as the secretary with orange hair returns to the other side of the desk.

Her lips are as orange as her hair, and her eyes are like a cat's, black in the center with a shimmering gold ring around the pupils.

"All right, Jude, I've been told that you should bring her back to the office," she informs the fire demon—Jude.

Then her cat eyes shake to me, and she eyes me over with puzzled intrigue.

Jude thrums his flame-tipped fingers against the desk. "Do they have an idea of why a human would end up here? Not that I actually believe she's human. Not with those eyes. Plus, she smells like magic. But she says she came from the human realm."

My eyes...

Wait... I smell like magic?

I sniff myself, but can't smell anything.

The cat-eyed secretary chuckles. Or well, more like purrs.

"No monster can smell their own scent," she says with a smile but then frowns. "Even a newbie should know that unless she doesn't know about our realm."

Jude frowns. "How would that be possible, though?"

"I'm not sure, but if she's been in the human realm for long enough, her powers may have been dormant. Or someone made them dormant. But if that's the case, then we're talking about a whole other set of problems." She fiddles with a bracelet on her wrist as she studies me quizzically.

And me? I just stand there stupidly, confusion swirling through me. And yet, beneath all the puzzlement, something is starting to click into place.

Is this why I've always felt so different and out of place?

"Yeah, you're right," Jude murmurs, observing me. "Tell me Haven, while you lived in the human realm, did you experiencing anything magical?"

"Other than the giant vortex that appeared and sucked me here?" I reply with a shrug. "Although, I'm still pretty convinced that was just a dream—that this whole thing is."

"Oh honey, this is very much reality." He taps his finger against his lips, making the flesh sizzle. "But the question is, how do you fit in here? And why did you end up here?"

"Well, if I'm not dreaming, then a woman with pink hair pushed me into the vortex," I explain. "Or well, according to her, she was a witch."

The cat-eyed woman's expression plummets. "A pink-haired witch sent you here?"

I nod, adjusting the handle of my backpack higher onto my shoulder. "Or well, she pushed me into the vortex that led to here… Wherever here is."

"I already told you, you're at Monster Academy for the Magical," Jude murmurs, lost in deep thought. He glances at the woman with cat eyes, a frown etching across his face. "If Annabella sent her here, then more than likely…"

"She needs to be protected," she finishes for him. "But the question is: why?"

They grow quiet, their gazes dissecting me. I have no idea what they're looking for, but it's making me very squirmy.

Eventually, Jude sighs. "Come with me, lovely grey-eyed Haven," he says. "And we'll figure out the mystery of your appearance here."

I expect him to walk to another door, but instead, he snaps his fingers, and a cloud of purple smoke encloses around me.

Nope. Not encloses around me.

Grabs me.

And just like that, I'm back in the darkness again.

I gasp, stumbling forward as the smoke releases me. "Holy crap, that was..." My words fade as I get a glimpse of my surroundings.

I'm no longer in the main dungeon, but a small, dark, and dingy room. With the cement walls, lack of windows and lighting, and muggy air, I assume Jude has finally taken me to a real dungeon.

"You don't need to be afraid." Jude materializes beside me in a puff of smoke, his fire-like eyes illuminating against the darkness. "This is just the headmistress's and headmaster's office."

I raise my brows. "It looks an awful lot like a dungeon."

He chuckles. "You're amusing, Haven. You really are."

Glad he thinks so, but I wasn't really trying to be amusing.

"What're we doing here?" I ask as Jude strolls around the room, eyeing the crooked paintings on the wall that are covered in cobwebs.

"Trying to figure out what you are and why you're here." He glances at me from over his shoulder. "I know you said that you don't know anything about this realm, but I can't help noticing how calm you are, so—and please don't take this personally—but..." He turns to face me, scrutinizing me with his smoldering eyes. "Are you sure you don't know what you are or why Annabella sent you here? Because it's okay if you do. I'd just rather know now instead of finding out later that you're lying."

I wonder what he'd do if I said I had been lying this entire time, that I know why I'm here, what I am...

What are you? The pink-haired witch—Annabella had said to me the first time I ran into her.

I had always wondered the same thing.

"I'm not lying," I tell him. "And honestly, I'm half-convinced this is all just a dream. That really, I'm asleep back in my bed. Or in a trance in the basement..." I bite down on my tongue, not wanting to talk about that.

His brows furrow. "Trance in the basement... what do you mean by that?"

I shrug, staring down at a puddle on the ground. "Nothing really. It's just that sometimes I go into trances.

It doesn't always happen while I'm in a basement, though. That's just where I was the last time it happened."

Concern masks his expression. "So you've gone into trances a lot?"

"It's happened a handful of times." I lift my gaze to him. "I'm not crazy, though. I swear I'm not."

"I never said you were, honey." He stares at me like I'm a complicated puzzle he desperately wants to solve. "What happens during these trances?"

I lift my shoulder. Usually, I'd keep my lips zipped, fearing I'll sound crazy. But this place... Well, it seems like the sort of place where crazy might be more accepted than sane.

"I zone out," I admit. "And then it's like... Well, like darkness grabs hold of me and then I black out."

"Do strange things happen to others around you when you go into these trances?" he asks cautiously.

I pick at my fingernail, shrugging. "I've been told I mumble words in a language no one seems to know, and my eyes go black, but..." I wrap my arms around myself. "The last time it happened, when I woke up, my foster father was cowering under the stairway, rambling in a weird language. And it happened another time when I was six, only that time it was my foster mother it happened to."

The crease between his brows deepens. "I'm assuming your foster parents were near you when you entered the trance?" he asks and I nod. "What events happened that lead up to you going into a trance?"

I smash my lips together and shake my head. "I don't want to talk about that."

Sympathy fills his eyes. "That's perfectly fine." He gives a brief pause. "I can tell this is bothering you, so I'll let the subject drop for now, but I just want to ask you one final question. And it's very important that you answer honestly, okay?" He waits for me to nod before continuing. "Did anything else happen to your foster parents while you were in a trance? Like did their skin get covered by flames or something like that?"

"No, nothing like that happened. But the last time… my foster father had these black lines covering his flesh."

The moment the words leave my lips, every flame and ember on his body fizzles, leaving him looking like a shadow.

"Oh dear Gods," he breathes out.

Puzzlement webs through me. I'm about to ask what's gotten him so worried when a man and woman materialize in the middle of the room.

The man is freakishly tall with hair and eyes as grey as ash. He's wearing a floor-length white cloak that trails behind him, and red lipstick stains the collar. Coincidentally enough—although, probably not coincidentally—the woman beside him has the same shade of lipstick smudged around her lips. Her hair is the same shade as the lipstick, along with the horns sprouting out of her head, and the red pops against the all-black outfit she's sporting.

"Good afternoon, everyone." The man claps his hands together, causing an eerie glow to orb around the room. A smile spreads across his face until he glances around. Then he frowns. "I thought this was a meeting?" He looks at the woman standing beside him.

"Not a meeting. There's an issue we need to address." She looks from Jude to me, her expression unreadable. "I'm assuming you're it."

Uncertain how to respond, I just shrug.

She frowns, a drop of annoyance flickering in her eyes.

"Sorry, Sage, she's a little confused," Jude tells her as he steps toward me. But then he abruptly slams to a stop, tension rippling through his body as he stares at me.

And that's when I notice it. That same fear I sometimes see in people's eyes after I've had one of my trances.

"Confused how?" Sage asks Jude.

He clears his throat then looks at her. "Did Camille fill you in on what happened?"

"No," the man replies, adjusting the collar of his cloak. "We've been busy with—"

Sage reaches over and squeezes his hand, her gaze remaining on Jude. "I've been made aware that an accidental arrival occurred and that the creature isn't certain why she's here."

"Creature?" I don't mean to say the word aloud, and the noise draws all of their attention.

"Yes, creature," Sage says to me with either annoyance or curiosity in her tone—she's difficult to read in a very creepy way. "Or were you not aware of that either?"

"She wasn't," Jude answers for me. "She's not aware of a lot of things."

Sage glances at him with her brow raised. "Then why is she here?"

"That's what I wanted to find out." Jude faces her with his hands behind his back. "It's why I asked for you to meet me here—so I could get your help trying to figure out why she's here and what she is. However, after talking to her for the last couple of minutes, I may have arrived at a conclusion." He grows stiff then, the flames in his body flickering.

His reaction causes tension to pour through me. I'm not sure what he's about to say if I even believe any of this or not, but I have a feeling something terrible is about to occur.

Now might be a good time to run.

I sneak a glance around, searching for an escape, but the room doesn't even have a door.

"I think... Well, considering some of the stuff she

said…" Jude opens and flexes his hands. "I think she might be a maddening."

I don't know what I expected him to say, but that wasn't it, that he'd say some word I don't know the meaning of. But Sage and the man seem to understand, both of them stiffening, their gazes sliding to me.

"You think she's a maddening?" the man questions in a low, tremulous tone, his grey eyes shadowing over.

Sage clutches onto his hand. "Mor, please calm down."

His gaze snaps to her, and black-feathered wings suddenly snap out from his back, causing feathers to scatter through the air.

I gape at him.

Wings?

This dude has *wings?*

Then he seems to grow twice his size, his body stretching taller the more his anger builds. "Calm down!" he shouts, and I stumble back, tripping over my feet and landing on my ass. "A maddening has been brought into the academy, and all you can say to me is calm down!"

I have to give Sage some credit as she stands there looking completely calm and maybe even a little bored.

"Oh, quit throwing a tizzy fit," she says with a roll of her eyes. "She clearly doesn't know what she is, which probably means her powers are mostly dormant."

Mor's nostrils flare as he gets in her face. "Mostly dormant or not, we don't allow her kind in this academy."

Sage crosses her arms. "That might be true, but the fact is she's already here, which means she's not going anywhere for the next year."

"Wait, what?" I ask, getting to my feet and looking at Jude.

He offers me an apologetic look. "It's the rules of the academy. Once you start the school year here, you're stuck with us for the next year, whether you want to or not. It helps keep the attendance rate up, which keeps the funding amount up."

"I…" I don't know what to say.

I try to latch onto to the hope that this really is a dream and that I'll wake up soon.

And that hope only grows when Mor fastens his gaze on me and says, "Take her to the dungeons. She can spend the next year there."

For a split second, I actually believe Jude and Sage are going to follow through with Mor's order. I start to back away, figuring I'll try to use my powers to get out of here. Not that I know what those powers are. But maybe, somehow, I can make a door appear…

Nope. All that happens when I stare into empty space, trying to conjure up a door with my brainpower, is I get a pounding headache.

"We're not taking her to the dungeons," Sage states and I can practically hear the eye roll through her voice. "We have plenty of dangerous creatures here—it's what we're known for."

"A maddening isn't just dangerous," Mor warns in a low tone, his wings shaking. "They're deadly."

A chill spills across my flesh. Deadly? They think I'm

deadly?

"So are vampires. And death angels. And dark faeries," Sage replies with a pressing look.

"If you're implying that me letting The Death Triplets into our academy was a mistake, then maybe I should remind you of how much funding we received from their parents," Mor bites out in annoyance.

"That doesn't make them any less dangerous," Sage stresses, crossing her arms.

Mor's wings expand wider, nearly reaching half the length of the room. "Maddenings are far more dangerous than The Death Triplets combined."

Sage cocks a brow. "Should I pull out their file and remind you of all the not-so-dangerous crap the Death Triplets have pulled while attending here?"

Mor grinds his teeth as he breathes in and out. Then just as quickly as he freaked out, he composes, his wings folding back underneath his cloak. "So you think we should let her attend here, then?"

Sage flicks a glance in my direction then looks back at Mor. "If we're able to properly train a maddening, imagine what it will do for our academy's reputation? And she seems like she could potentially be trainable. Although, we'll have to look more into her background and find out where she came from." She fastens her gaze on me. "You're from the human realm, correct?" she asks and I nod. "What were you doing while you lived there?"

"I…" I give a nervous shrug. "Bouncing through foster homes pretty much."

She steps toward me, her heels clicking against the cement. "And you don't know who your parents are?"

I shake my head.

She chews on her lip. "How did you end up here?"

"She was pushed into a vortex by Annabella," Jude answers for me, stepping up beside me, yet keeping a bit of distance, a move I assume has to do with me being one of these dangerous maddening creatures.

Please let this be a dream…

Then again, is going back to foster homes any better?

"One of our huntresses," Sage murmurs, her gaze boring into me. "We should probably summon Annabella and see what she knows about this and why she sent the maddening here." She pauses for a beat before straightening her stance. "Until then, lets get Haven settled in and get her set up with a guide who can explain everything to her. I'd also like you to assist her too, when necessary," she directions this statement to Jude. "She knows absolutely nothing about our realm and our ways, so she's going to require extra attention."

"I can do that," Jude tells her with a slight bow of his head, the flames in his body igniting again. "But do you have a specific guide in mind?"

Sage taps her fingertip against her red lips, silence stretching by as she considers Jude's question.

"We should assign the Death Triplets to her," Mor says, plucking a feather from his hair.

I frown, recalling how hazy my mind had felt while I was around the three guys… creatures. Not to mention I suck when it comes to being around guys. Well, not so much guys but people in general.

Then again, no one here is actually human…

Oh my God.

Reality bitch slaps me across the face.

"Holy crap, I think this is real," I breathe out.

"You think that's a good idea?" Sage asks Mor with hesitancy written across her face, either not hearing what I said or just not caring.

Mor's gaze strays to me then back to her. "You know as well as I do that many students aren't going to be accepting of her once they find out what she is."

"Yes, but we can always keep that hidden for as long as possible," Sage replies. "In fact, it might be for the best for now if very little students and teachers know what she is."

"I agree," Mor says. "However, her guides should probably be made aware of her situation and be accepting of it. And considering what the Death Triplets are, I think they might be our best bet."

Sage scratches her horn. "Perhaps. But do we really want to risk the Death Triplets turning into the Death Quadruplets?"

"Whatever group she's part of, she'll pose the same amount of risk," Mor stresses. "At least this way, she'll be surrounded by creatures that can handle her..." He casts a wary glance at me. "Intense abilities."

Intense abilities? Just exactly what can I do?

I think about Mia and Tim and what happened to them when I felt that darkness purring under my skin.

What are my powers?

Sage gives a nod, strands of her red hair falling into her eyes. "You're probably right. I just hope this doesn't turn into a disaster."

"I do too," Mor agrees with a frown. But then he shakes his head and turns to face me. "All right, Haven Wyllowravelee, do you have any questions before we assign you to your guides?"

Do I have any questions? Is he freakin' kidding me?"

"Yeah," I answer nervously. "What exactly is this academy for? And what's a Maddening? What can they do exactly? And what am I going to be learning while I attend here?"

The room grows so silent you can hear the shuffling of Mor's feathers underneath his cloak.

"I'll handle this," Jude says to Sage and Mor, lifting his blazing arm in front of him and sending smoke swirling through the air.

"Thank you, Jude," Sage says then looks at me. "I want you to understand what a great honor it is to attend this academy. Do not take that lightly, okay?" She doesn't wait for me to respond, turning to Mor. "Ready to get back to business?"

Mor gives her a grin that makes me wonder what sort of business they're going back to, if it has anything to do with why Mor has lipstick on the collar of his cloak.

Then just as abruptly as they materialized, they dissipate into thin air. And I'm left standing there, speechless, and so freakin' confused.

Story of my life, I guess. Only this is way, way different than just being a socially awkward girl in the human world that everyone seems afraid of.

Jude sticks out his flame-y hand for me to take. "Come along, honey. Let's go get you checked in. And while we do, I'll try to explain some things to you. And prepare you for the Death Triplets. Although you handled them well earlier, so I'm not too worried."

Part of me doesn't want to take his hand, feels like the second I do, my life will forever change. But honestly, my life wasn't that great to begin with. So I place my hand in his, crossing my fingers that whatever is waiting for me in this new life will be better than what I had in the human world.

But considering what Mor and Sage said about me supposedly deadly…

Yeah, I'm a bit worried that I might be worse off in this new monster life.

Jude and I leave the office the same way we entered —through a cloud of smoke. When I ask what the crap it is, Jude explains to me that the smoke is a magical form of transportation, that everything in the academy is magical.

"But you have to have access to that magic," he explains as we make our way down a narrow, dimly lit hallway paved with cobblestone. "And you won't have access to that until you're a third year."

We're headed to dorm area where I'll get checked in and be assigned a room, classes, etc. From what Jude has told me about the academy, it sounds similar to private prep schools. Only this school is run by magic, is located in the Moonlight realm, and only monsters with magical bloodlines are allowed to attend, like vampires, fey, werewolves, shapeshifters, and a lot of other creatures I've never heard of, most of their titles ending with *demon.* Jude also informed me that the main goal of the academy is to train creatures to hunt down dangerous monsters that pose a threat to our realms. Monster hunters and huntresses, he called the creatures that graduate from the academy and get hired to go hunt dangerous creatures down. Like Annabella, the witch who shoved me into the vortex that brought me here, which leaves me wondering why she felt like I needed to be here and be protected.

"How many years do creatures go to this school?" I ask as I try to take in all of this.

It's complicated, though. Trying to believe everything I'm being told, everything that's happened, everything I'm seeing. Honestly, part of me is still convinced I'm in a nightmare. The only thing that has me questioning if perhaps this is real is that I've spent years wondering if I had some sort of magic ability.

"A total of three years." Jude's ember-like eyes slide to me. "How old are you now?"

"Seventeen," I say and he frowns. I tense. "Is that bad or something?"

He wavers. "Most monsters start here when they're sixteen, so you're a year behind. That's okay, though. You'll just graduate a bit late."

"If I stay here." I lower my hand to my side as I sigh.

"Mor and Sage made it sound like they weren't sure if they'd let me stay here for more than a year."

"It's nothing personal." His boots scuff against the floor as we slow to a stop in front of a fork in the hallway.

"It sounded personal," I mutter. "I mean, they basically don't want me here because I'm a maddening, which I still don't know what that is."

"It's not just because you're a maddening." He motions for me to take the left path that leads to a thick wooden door with various locks covering it. "The academy is known for accepting creatures from very prestigious families. And most of these families donate a lot of money." He stops in front of the door then turns to look at me. "Occasionally, we accept charity students, but those cases are rare."

"So am I supposed to be considered a charity student then?"

"Maybe… Honestly, I'm not sure what they're going to say about you. But like Sage and More said, it's very important you avoid telling others what kind of creature you are."

I release a stressed breath. "But what if someone asks?"

He wavers. "For now, just tell them you're a witch. We'll figure out something better before classes start."

I'm supposed to tell everyone I'm a witch?

So weird.

Then again, all of this is weird…

"When do classes start?" I tuck a strand of my hair behind my ear. "And what sort of classes will I be taking? And what am I even supposed to be learning?"

He chuckles, smoke hissing from his lips. "I'll tell you what. I'll download some info on a handheld for you to read that should explain a lot of that to you. And while I'm here to help you, I think the Death Triplets will be able to answer the questions you have related to your classes."

"Okay." I chew on my bottom lip as he reaches to unlock the door. "But you still haven't really told me what a maddening is."

He pauses mid-reach. "I know. I know." He sighs, lowering his hand. "I've been procrastinating that part, but I guess I probably need to tell you before I let you walk into the dorm." He rakes his flame-kissed fingers through his fiery hair. "A maddening is a very, *very* rare creature that a lot of other creatures fear, mostly because their powers can become deadly, depending on which path the maddening chooses to take."

I swallow the lump wedged in my throat. "Are maddenings the only creatures with deadly powers?"

He shakes his head, but then hesitates. "But they're one of the few creatures that can kill just by a touch. And the kind of death they inflict…" He releases a smoky exhale. "With a simple touch, maddenings can curse a creature—or person—to go insane. And when they decide to use their powers to kill, they sentence the person or creature to a torturous after-death, their soul sent down to the Underworld, which is a realm ran by Shadow Demons. And those demons thrive on torturing souls. So if a maddening decides to kill a creature with their powers, they're sentencing that creature to an eternity of painful torture."

"Oh." That's all I say—can say.

My chest feels tight, like I can't quite breathe properly.

"But that's only if the maddening chooses to go down that path," Jude stresses. "You don't have to choose that path, Haven. And from what I've seen so far, I don't believe you will."

"I won't," I assure him.

But I can't help thinking about Tim and Mia and how for a brief moment, I wanted to hurt them. How I had felt some sort of darkness stirring inside me when the thought flickered through my mind.

But I decide to keep that to myself since everyone already seems edgy around me.

"Is there anything else I can do?" I ask as Jude reaches for the locks.

He shakes his head, but avoids my gaze, making me question if he's lying. "No, not really."

"Oh." I watch as he begins to twist and unblock the locks, feeling nervous and restless, tons of questions cramming my mind. But one in particular is begging to be asked. "You said that maddenings are rare… Will that… I mean, if I try, could I be able to find my parents?"

He rubs his lips together, reluctance flashing across his face. "I don't want to upset you, but I feel like I should probably be honest with this." He rotates a clock-shaped lock and gadgets inside the door click. "Maddenings are very rare because they're usually killed, either out of fear or because they've committed a crime. And since you were living in the human realm as an orphan…" He swallows hard, not finishing.

But I get the gist of what he's saying.

"My parents are probably dead," I say quietly.

All of my life, I assumed my parents didn't want me. Never did I think they had given me up because they died.

"I'm sorry." Jude offers me a sympathetic look. "I know this is a lot to take in, and I wish I could say it'll get easier, but for a while, things might be intense. Hopefully, though, once you've learned more about this realm, this school, and what it means to be a monster, things will get better. I also think it'll help once we start looking into your background. Maybe then, you'll be able to get some answers about where you come from."

I nod, but my chest remains tight.

My parents are probably dead.

I really am alone.

Jude forces a smile onto his face. "On the bright side, though, you do get to live in one of our best dorm rooms in the academy."

Before I ask why, he shoves the door open.

On the other side is an enormous room with a high peaked ceiling lit up by a chandelier woven of thorns. The walls are brick and covered in alcoves, and purple rug is spread across the floor. A velvet set of chairs is in the center of the room, and a flat-screen television is hanging on the farthest wall, which seems like the most out of place item this place.

So monsters watch television? Weird...

"Where are the beds?" I wonder as I follow Jude into the room.

He points to various arched doorways. "There's one in each of these, along with a kitchen and two bathrooms."

"Oh." I shake my head in astonishment. "Are all the dorm rooms this fancy?"

"Gods know." He laughs. "Most of them look a lot like the Headmaster and Headmistress's office."

I step further into the room, taking it all in. "Why's this one so fancy then?"

"Because this room belongs to the Death Triplets," Jude explains, a handheld device appearing in the palm of his hand. "They come from some of the wealthiest families, who donate a lot of money to the academy. And in return, they get all of this." He gives a gesture around the room as he glances at the screen of the handheld device.

"I guess that makes sense," I say, confusion rising inside me. "But I thought you said this was my dorm room?"

He bobs his head up and down. "It is."

Something dawns on me then.

Something that makes me very uneasy.

"Wait... Does that mean—"

"That you'll have the pleasure of being our room-mate." The guy with blue hair and fangs that I saw earlier cuts me off as he ambles into the room.

Phoenix, I think his name is. And from what I'm guessing, a vampire.

Holy crap, this dude is a vampire.

Again, reality throat punches me like a little bitch.

I'm in a place where vampires and other monsters exist—where magic exists. And I'm part of this realm, a deadly, rare creature. After seventeen years of living a life where I always felt completely out of place and believing I was a freak, it finally makes sense. I felt that way because I wasn't human. I wasn't really just a freak.

And now...

Well, now I'm not sure what I am or where I fit in. Will other creatures accept me here if they don't know what I really am?

I guess I'll find out.

"I have to share a dorm room with three guys?" I ask Jude, resisting a frown.

But seriously, sharing a dorm with three guys, one of who's a vampire? Sure, I've shared rooms with guys before, during my stays in foster homes that broke the rules. But this is different. This dorm room is way more private. Not to mention these aren't really guys, but powerful monsters.

I try to recall what Sage referred to them as. A vampire, which is probably Phoenix, at least his fangs suggest so. Sage also mentioned a dark faerie and a death angel.

"Don't seem so upset about it," Phoenix mocks me with a smirk. "Most girls—hell, most creatures would die to be in your position right now."

Great. He's a cocky jerk. Not that I didn't suspect that already.

Good thing I've dealt with assholes before, built skin of steel to deal with it—to deal with way, way worse stuff. Although, usually, I try to walk away from the situation. Living with the cocky jerk, though… Yeah, I won't be able to walk away a lot.

"Good for them." I cross my arms, hoping I appear more confident than I feel. "But personally, I'd rather just live in a regular dorm room."

His ruby eyes glimmer. "Is that so?"

My heart thunders in my chest, but I remain calm on the outside. "Yep."

His smirk widens. "Well, aren't you just positively delicious?"

My heart rate quickens. Does he mean that metaphorically?

"Phoenix, knock it off." The guy with dark hair, grey eyes, and shadows dancing across his skin enters the room—Roman, if I remember correctly.

He looks different than when I saw him in the throne room, less shadowy.

Phoenix sinks his fangs into his bottom lip, his gaze remaining welded to me. "What? All I said was that she's absolutely delicious? Which she is."

I fight back the urge to step away from him. "No, I'm not."

Clearly, that's the wrong thing to say, something I learn when Phoenix's grin broadens.

"Why don't you come over here so I can find out for myself?" he purrs, tracing his tongue along the tips of his fangs as he steps closer to me.

"Um..." Jude clears his throat, startling the hell out of me.

Shit, I forgot he was here. Maybe because Phoenix was doing that hazing thing to me again?

I narrow my eyes at Phoenix, but he only grins.

"Delicious," he murmurs.

"I assume you've been informed that you'll be taking Haven under your wing," Jude says to Phoenix.

Phoenix doesn't remove his gaze off of me, even when Roman steps between us.

"Yes, we've been given instructions to take care of her." Roman steps closer to Jude and Jude's flames begin to fizzle. "You can go now. We'll handle it from here."

I throw Jude a pleading look—I don't even know why. It's not like I've known him for very long, but I don't want to be left alone with these guys. It's kind of a weird move for me to seek help from someone else, seeing as how I'm used to handling stuff on my own. But this is different. Everything about this time, moment, place is different.

"*Sorry,*" Jude mouths to me as he backs toward the door. "If you need anything at all, just send me a message."

I gape at him. Is he really leaving me alone with these guys? "On what—"

Poof.

Smoke funnels from my palm as a handheld device appears in my hand.

I blink at it then back at Jude only to find him gone, the smell of singed ash lingering in the air.

My fingers curl around the handheld device, my pulse soaring. I haven't felt this anxious since the first time I was dropped off at a group home. I was six, and up until then, I had been living in foster homes. I was so terrified of being somewhere different, of the unknown. And on my first day there, I went into a trance while I was being introduced to some of the other kids. That had me instantly labeled a freak, and I was tormented because of it, a couple of girls even cutting off my hair while I slept. I spent days crying to myself about it, which led to even more ridicule and torment. And that made me despise group homes. At least it did then. But as time moved on, and I experienced the darker side of life, I discovered that getting my hair cut off was mild compared to other punishments, and that group homes weren't nearly as bad as I had initially thought. I also learned how to deal with the unknown better, started weaving my skin with that metaphoric steel.

You can handle this, Haven. It's just a couple of guys.

Of course, my little mental pep talk becomes irrelevant as the third party of the Death Triplets strolls into the room—Ollie, I think his name is.

He doesn't say anything, his pale gaze simply gobbling me up as he studies me. "You're very pretty for a maddening," he states with a hint of curiosity. "Although, I've never actually seen one before."

"Then how do you know I'm not ugly for one?" I find myself saying, again acting completely out of character for me.

But I don't like being assessed this closely. Usually,

people look the other way whenever I'm around, like they're afraid to meet my gaze. The last person I crossed paths with that did make eye contact with me, and for far too long I might add, was Tim.

I cringe at the reminder of my foster father.

"Huh, I've never seen that before," Phoenix muses, rubbing his jawline, his gaze skating to Ollie. "She's completely disgusted with you."

Ollie rolls his eyes. "If she's disgusted, it definitely has to do with you."

Phoenix's bloodstained lips quirk as he steps toward Ollie. "Not likely. Vampires are way too alluring. Dark fey on the other hand…" He flashes his fangs.

Well, that answers my question about what kind of creatures they are.

The tips of Ollie's fingertips spark. Actually freaking spark, like sparklers.

"Will you two stop arguing for one damn minute and focus on the problem we discussed?" Roman intervenes with heavy annoyance.

"Oh, yeah, right." Ollie tears his gaze off of Phoenix, the sparks on his fingers dimming as he looks at me again.

All of them do.

I fight back the urge to gulp. "Why are you guys looking at me like that?"

Ollie lifts a shoulder while Phoenix smirks. And

Roman? His gaze darkens, those shadows on his skin appearing.

"You know, I'm surprised Sage and Mor assigned you to us." Roman steps toward me, his thick boots scuffing against the floor. "Considering my family's history with maddenings." He stops in front of me, and I fight back the urge to step back. "I can't decide it if was intentional, if they wanted to place you with a creature who would instantly hate you, or if they're just stupid. Honestly, with Mor, it could be either. Sage has always seemed smarter than that, though. But maybe she was distracted by Mor."

Ollie snickers at that and Phoenix elbows him in the side.

"Dude." Ollie winces as he targets a dirty look at Phoenix, who simply rolls his eyes.

"Look at me when I'm talking to you," Roman demands, hooking his finger underneath my chin and forcing me to look at him.

That's when my tongue becomes unstuck from the roof of my mouth. Well, either that or the hazing thing these guys can cause lifts from my mind.

I jerk my chin away from him, hoping to appear more confident than I feel. "Just because you're supposed to be guiding me around this school doesn't mean you can boss me around… I'm tired of being bossed around."

A shadow casts across Roman's face as he leans in, his breath dusting across my face. "I'm sure you are," he says in a low tone that makes chills break out across my skin. "Your kind usually do most of the bossing around. Almost as much as they like killing other creatures."

I sense then that this has more to do with him just being a jerk. He hates my kind for some reason.

"And I'm not about to let some killer come into my group and hurt my friends," he adds, anger blazing in his shadowy eyes.

"I'm not a killer," I tell him, loathing how shaky my tone has gotten.

"Liar," he says lowly. "Your kind always cause pain and death wherever you go."

I shake my head, but my thoughts drift to what I did to Tim and Mia.

I wonder if it's permanent, if what I did to them will ever wear off.

"So, here's what we're going to do." Roman leans away from me, going from intense to calm in the snap of a finger. "We're going to make sure you never get a chance to hurt anyone."

Then he lifts his hand and Ollie and Phoenix move in around me.

Okay, this is so bad.

I reel around to run, but Ollie zips around behind me, moving at an inhuman speed.

"Oh, no you don't." He shoves me forward, sending me stumbling into Roman's arms.

The force causes me to drop the handheld device Jude gave me, and my backpack falls off my arms.

Before I can recover, Roman shoves me back, but his fingers wrap around my wrist so I can't go very far.

For the briefest moment, I feel like Tim is pinning me down against the floor again. But then I snap out of it and move to kick Roman.

"Easy," he warns, blocking my kick. "The more you fight, the worse this'll be."

"Doubtful," I snap, trying to shove him.

But he holds onto me with his freakishly strong grip.

"Let me go," I growl out.

And then I feel it, that darkness purring inside my veins.

Hurt them.

"Hurry up," Roman bites out, his fingers tensing on my wrist. "Before she ends up killing me."

"I'm not going to kill you," I snap, struggling to get away from him. "I'm not a killer."

Hatred burns in his eyes. "Look at you. You've got killer written all over you. Literally."

"No, I don't..." The words fade from my tongue as I catch a glimpse of my arms.

Like the other day, my veins have become more prominent and are protruding underneath my flesh.

"What's happening to me?" I whisper in horror.

For a flicker of an instant, Roman's brows knit in confusion.

But then he hastily erases the look and shouts, "Do it!"

A bright blue light suddenly illuminates around the room then heat blasts through the air, so potent I have to close my eyes.

What was that?

Am I dead?

I breathe in and out as the air settles down again. Then I crack open my eyes.

I...

What the...

I shake my head in shock... and in anger.

While Roman is no longer holding onto me, I still can't move from where I stand because a cage now surrounds me.

"Let me out of here," I growl, gripping the bars.

Ollie and Phoenix smirk at me from the other side while Roman watches me with a guarded expression.

"Not a chance, sweetheart," Ollie says to me with a grin.

I lock eyes with Roman. "I don't know what happened with the other maddening you met, but I'm not a killer."

"I guess we'll see, won't we?" He steps forward and pats the bar. "If deep down inside you, you aren't then eventually the bars of this cage will melt away. However, if the magic laced in these bars sense you're evil, the cage will remain in place until it can feel otherwise." He gives me a cold, cruel smile. "My bet is you'll be the new decoration to our room for a very, very long time."

With that, he steps back, and they all head toward the door.

I rattle the bars. "Let me out!"

They ignore me, exiting the room and shutting the door behind them.

And just like that, I become trapped again, like I was in Tina and Tim's basement. Only this time, I might not ever get out.

"No." I shake my head as I sink to the ground. "I'm not a killer." I stare at the bars, willing them to understand that, willing them to melt away.

But they remain in place, keeping me trapped, and letting me know that maybe, just maybe, somewhere deep inside me, I might be a killer.

Part of me feels bad for locking her up. I hate that I feel that way. I shouldn't feel bad at all. She's a killer, whether she's killed yet or not. Her kind always ends up killing, causing death wherever they go, just like the one I met.

"So how are we going to keep this hidden from that fire demon?" Ollie asks as we wander the hallways of the academy.

School doesn't start for another week, so hardly anyone has arrived yet. The only reason Ollie, Phoenix, and I are here is because we chose to come here early. It sounds a bit strange, but it's either come to school early and hang out with each other or spend more time in our homes, by ourselves, because none of our parents are around much. It comes with the territory of coming from a darker bloodline. The darkness inside us makes us more cold, distant, and uncaring. At least that's what I was always told.

When I was younger, I used to be a nice kid. I'd share my toys with others. When I attended the all-death-angels academy, I was the best flyer in my class, and I spent time trying to teach others to fly as well as me. But when my father found out about that, he taught me a lesson. And by lesson, I mean he beat me until I promised I'd become the cold, cruel creature he wanted me to be.

"Emotions will ruin you," he told me as he struck me across the face. "Do you want to end up feeling things for the rest of your life? Do you want to let others control you? Be able to break you?"

I had shaken my head. He made it sound so awful.

After that, I started fighting against my kind instincts. And now here I am, part of a group everyone calls the Death Triplets. Creatures fear us. Flee when we come around. And that's the way we like it.

At least, that's what we tell everyone.

"We'll figure it out later," I tell Ollie, pulling myself from my thoughts.

"Maybe she'll get out," Phoenix remarks, stuffing his hands into his pockets.

I shake my head. "She won't."

Phoenix glances at me. "I don't know, man... Honestly, she didn't seem that scary."

I glare at him. "She's a maddening. That cage will never let her out."

But deep down, in that tiny, good part of me that just won't seem to die, I want Haven to get out. But it's a naïve hope. Like I said before, all maddenings are killers. I know this first hand, learned it the day one of them killed my brother and sister with their cold, darkness-filled, murderous hands.

CHAPTER 13

"Your performance was flawless," Mor said to his colleague and lover.

"Of course it was." Sage turned from the window, dabbing a bit of smeared lipstick on her face. "Everything I do is flawless."

She was right. Everything about her perfection, from the way she smiled to how talented she was at manipulating a situation. She was a succubus, though, which are known for their perfection, whether it be real or not.

Sometimes Mor wondered if she was manipulating him, if their secret relationship was nothing more than a con. After all, the two of them didn't really make any sense. He was an old, worn-out shapeshifter who had been stuck in the form of a storm angel for quite some time after his powers had weakened due to a spell cast upon him. Before that, he had been confident, strong, and nearly perfect. But now he felt withered and tired. He looked the part too.

"Yes, I know." Mor sank back in his chair and lit up his pipe, watching Sage return her attention to the dew-kissed window.

She seemed distracted today, and it bothered him that he couldn't figure out why.

"Tell me again why we're doing this," he said as he puffed on the pipe. "Why we brought a maddening here. This school was doing just fine without one living behind our walls."

"This school was dying, Mor," she stated with her arms crossed. "We're getting less and less funding every year as more of our students are dropping out and attending academies that focus on less dangerous jobs. And that low graduation rate means we have fewer huntresses and hunters protecting our realms. The death rates have already spiked, and this coming year is supposed to be even worse unless we can recruit more students."

"I guess you're right," Mor muttered. "I still don't quite understand, though, why having a maddening at the academy will help more students graduate?"

"Because it'll make the academy more appealing." She ambled toward him, swaying her hips. "Imagine the reputation we'll get if we can train her to become a huntress—if we can train a maddening?"

He guessed he could see her point. Still, he felt like there was more to it than what she was telling him. He knew she had been looking for a maddening for a while, and when she discovered Haven in the human realm, she had sent Annabella to collect her, but she didn't want anyone knowing that part of the story.

"We need to pretend we found her by accident," Sage had told Mor when she informed him of her plan.

He had agreed then without much hesitation. Now, though, he wished he had asked more questions. Maybe he would have if she hadn't distracted him with her many… talents.

"Are you sure there's not more to this than what you're telling me?" he asked again, trying to focus on the conversation and past her wonderful succubus scent.

"Of course." She smiled at him then straddled his waist, took the pipe from his hand, and set it down on the table. "Why would I lie to you?" She combed her fingers through his hair. "When I love you?"

Then she lowered her lips to his and Mor completely forgot about everything else. And that's just how Sage wanted it.

Jessica Sorensen is a *New York Times* and *USA Today* best-selling author who lives in the snowy mountains of Wyoming. When she's not writing, she spends her time reading and hanging out with her family.

Also by Jessica Sorensen

Monster Academy for the Magical:

Monster Academy for the Magical

Monster Academy for the Magical: The Monster Trial (coming soon)

Signed with a Kiss

Accepting the Deal

Untitled (coming soon)

My Life with the Band:

Discovering Benton

Untitled (coming soon)

Honeyton Annabella Series:

The Illusion of Annabella

Untitled (coming soon)

Rebels & Misfits:

Confessions of a Kleptomaniac

Untitled (coming soon)

Enchanted Chaos Series:

Enchanted Chaos

Shimmering Chaos

Untitled (coming soon)

The Breathing Undead Series:

Breathing Lies

Shadowed Whisperers (coming soon)

My Cursed Superhero Life:

Cursed

Untitled (coming soon)

Capturing Magic:

Chasing Wishes

Chasing Magic

Untitled (coming soon)

Chasing the Harlyton Sisters Series:

Chasing Hadley

Falling for Hadley

Holding onto Hadley

Untitled (coming soon)

Tangled Realms:

Forever Violet

Forever Stardust

Untitled (coming soon)

Curse of the Vampire Queen:

Tempting Raven

Enchanting Raven

Alluring Raven

Untitled (coming soon)

Unraveling You Series:

Unraveling You

Raveling You

Awakening You

Inspiring You

Every Single Breath

Untitled (coming soon)

Unexpected Series:

The Unexpected Complications of Revenge

Untitled (coming soon)

Shadow Cove Series:

What Lies in the Darkness

What Lies in the Dark

Untitled (coming soon)

Mystic Willow Bay Series:

The Secret Life of a Witch

Broken Magic

Stolen Kisses

One Wild, Crazy, Zombie Night

Magical Whispers & the Undead

Untitled (coming soon)

Standalones:

The Forgotten Girl

The Heartbreaker Society:

The Opposite of Ordinary

The Heartbreaker Society Curse (coming soon)

Broken City Series:

Nameless

Forsaken

Oblivion

Forbidden (coming soon)

Guardian Academy Series:

Entranced

Entangled

Enchanted

Entice

The Forest of Shadow and Bones

Untitled (coming soon)

Sunnyvale Series:

The Year I Became Isabella Anders

The Year of Falling in Love

The Year of Second Chances

Untitled (coming soon)

The Coincidence Series:

The Coincidence of Callie and Kayden

The Redemption of Callie and Kayden

The Destiny of Violet and Luke

The Probability of Violet and Luke

The Certainty of Violet and Luke

The Resolution of Callie and Kayden

Seth & Greyson

The Evermore of Callie & Kayden

Untitled (coming soon)

The Secret Series:

The Prelude of Ella and Micha

The Secret of Ella and Micha

The Forever of Ella and Micha

The Temptation of Lila and Ethan

The Ever After of Ella and Micha

Lila and Ethan: Forever and Always

Untitled (coming soon)

Ella and Micha: Infinitely and Always

The Shattered Promises Series:

Shattered Promises

Fractured Souls

Unbroken

Broken Visions

Scattered Ashes

Breaking Nova Series:

Breaking Nova

Saving Quinton

Delilah: The Making of Red

Nova and Quinton: No Regrets

Tristan: Finding Hope

Wreck Me

Ruin Me

Untitled (coming soon)

The Fallen Star Series:

The Fallen Star

The Underworld

The Vision

The Promise

The Lost Soul

The Evanescence

The Darkness Falls Series:

Darkness Falls

Darkness Breaks

Darkness Fades

The Death Collectors Series (NA and YA):

Ember X and Ember

Cinder X and Cinder

Spark X and Spark

Unbeautiful Series:

Unbeautiful

Untamed